WORDS OF A SOUL

MIND AND INTERACTIONS WITH THE WORDS OF OTHERS

BY

SANJEEV KUMAR BHARADWAJ

pencil

ISBN 978-93-5438-617-6

© Sanjeev Kumar Bharadwaj 2020

Published in India 2020 by Pencil

A brand of

One Point Six Technologies Pvt. Ltd.

123, Building J2, Shram Seva Premises,

Wadala Truck Terminal, Wadala (E)

Mumbai 400037, Maharashtra, INDIA

E connect@thepencilapp.com

W www.thepencilapp.com

DISCLAIMER: *The opinions expressed in this book are those of the authors and do not purport to reflect the views of the Publisher.*

Author biography

I am Sanjeev Kumar Bharadwaj, a guy residing in Guwahati and with a desire to be somebody. A confused mind and a confused outlook towards life.

Apart from programming, writing has always been something that supported me while growing up, a confused life you may call it but being able to pen down things has made me understand myself. My own words confuse me and often I am left wondering what is it that I am even feeling. I am not old enough to lecture someone, nor old enough to be "experienced" but some things can happen even when you aren't old and you simply learn from them.

In my poems, there are confusions that I try to clear, situations that never made sense, and rhymes that never played out, but I read them all one day and it all made sense: that's when I started to realize what was going on with my mind and I became conscious. I am not there yet, but I am not far.

The poems are from the interactions with people, often when they shared with me their experiences of love, hate, reasons, or despair. Some are my own feelings, whereas some are the feelings of others through the words.

Be happy, You are a wonderful being :)

Contents

A thing

There this thing,
Thing called thoughts.
Imagining roughs and whatnot.
He tried to calm his mind.
Using all the means that he could find.
Words left out, completing them,
Building up stories, hurting himself somehow.
Oh, he wishes to be fine, to be what he can be, but
Unfinished words of some, stuck up thoughts
he needs to clear but wishes to bother not.
Sudden triggers closes in thta heavy heart,
He tries to go back where he was.
Fake a smile, Laugh a little while,
showing himself that he is fine.
No need to share as it brings out care,
Especially when there is none to hear.

Unknown Depth

The depth of darkness in his heart,

unknown to all but for him it lasts.

Thoughts and reasons aside,

all of his feelings collide.

Cofused and forsaken he remains,

for it is his mind that creates.

Emotions of hatred and envy,

clouds his world of beauty.

For he created his own reasons,

his greatest weapon has become his own prison.

Oddity

Isn't it odd,

When your mind plays games with you.

You understand everything, yet you deny it.

Clueless, pointless, and without feelings.

The end is near and that's what you feel,

but it's life and it keeps ongoing.

Till the final moments you understand nothing.

You know

Dear mine,

Do you know? Do you feel?

The emptiness inside and the unpleasant dream.

Do you understand that dream where

I am with you and I tell you what you mean.

I tell you how happy you made me,

which is more than I ever could be.

Ones where I ask you to be mine, and

I promise to be yours.

Yes, I do dream even if time is against me,

and my heart breaks indefinitely.

I do dream to accomplish, and

have you always beside me.

O dear mine,

I want nothing,

but sometimes do acknowledge me.

I got none and this heart is young.

A promise is to be kept,

but you forget me.

Gone

What's there? What's not?

It's simply all gone.

No more rhymes, no more poems

'cause the topic is now unknown.

Fear, anxiety, sadness all meanings dissolved.

Gone are those times and moments,

when words described the truth of love, and

eyes searched for you even in the crowd,

it still does but a lot lesser now.

For it all meant nothing to you, I believe.

Vast ocean of life and a drop I remain,

now it's hard to follow, to feel and understand.

What is true and what is false,

it all seems fake.

Momentart feel is what now all remains

Dearest

My dearest friend,

this is a letter to you,

my thoughts, your words.

Beautiful as always and true, I do miss you.

You aren't there anymore, but I shall always cherish you.

Oh, my loveliest friend, I sure miss you.

Hold my hand again, and I shall hold yours

Together we shall walk again, like the days before.

With nothing much to say, but with much to convey,

My beautiful friend, I shall always miss you.

In times I look for you,

believe me, I know you do too,

I sense you standing beside me always,

For you are my dearest friend, and

I miss you.

Wish

It's just a wish,

To hold someone in arms,

To feel being loved.

To have someone in my own tears,

And leave the world apart.

It's just a wish,

To feel alive with a kiss,

To hug someone, and

Feel happy and alive.

It's just a wish,

To sleep with someone hugging all night,

Feeling the happiness of other's breathe, every night.

Thinking of joys, sharing about the day all night.

Be in love, just by looking at each other's eyes.

Oh, it's just a wish, A wish.

Think of Me

Will anyone remember me when I am gone

From this world, beyond life,

when I close my eyes and

never get to wake up to see the next sunrise?

Will anyone think of me,

I don't have many memories,

Not much time spent creating moments with these.

I lay there thinking this,

when I felt my life slipping away so well.

I want to hold on to this life,

I want to be remembered when I am gone.

Lesser the time I have in hand, the growing fear I do feel.

I just want to live, as now I found my one,

One with whom I want to dream.

Doubts

Having his doubts,

confusions in his mind.

Looking at someone's past,

he stays awake this night.

Maybe he has a wrong perception, but

how can he trust someone for no reason?

He has experienced the bitter,

the pain and anger.

He doesn't want his present to result in the same, later.

Time flies by, so do people.

Words live forever, yet

hurts when left unbound.

Believe

Will you believe me, if I tell you

that I have lost my desire to be fine and to do good.

To be with anyone around, and to do things that I liked.

Will you believe me, if my reasons are null,

I find no purpose and no more fun.

Things that were interesting now seem dull.

Will you help me, if all above is true

and I extend my hand for yours, will you take mine too?

Will you give me a reason to be fine,

to feel properly and think properly and be me again?

Will you believe me,

For all might seem fine, but inside I cannot get through.

Will you believe me?

Unusual

Unusual the way he acts,

the ways by which he keeps his feelings suppressed.

He got everything, he wanted and

not much to complain about.

He got a good life with people to care and

not much to fear.

Yet, a void he feels, one that cannot be filled,

He doesn't know what he feels.

Thoughtless, he wants to be.

Mindless, he needs to be.

Fo the got everything yet, he feels unusual.

The way he need not be.

Selflessly Selfish

He who cared for all, and

Looked out for all,

never wanting the same for him.

Felt the sadness when an else felt,

for he knew the pain of being left out in the crowd.

He too once was the same,

carefree and selfish, lived for himself.

Looking out only for whatever was his, and

for him, she was his.

When she changed, he changed.

Now she doesn't feel for him, but for else.

For she taught him to live, and

Not just for self but for else.

Never think of what comes next,

"Be selfless, being selfish", she said.

Pointless

Loving you was the sweetest part,

Seeing you, made my heart fly.

Your eyes, your smile

One in a million, best in life.

You got bored of me, I didn't.

I just loved you, all day and night.

Reasons, made no sense,

Now love seems pointless.

Not Right

I lay awake tonight,

For the day it was sleepy and finer.

I lay awake tonight, thinking of you,

My love, my life, everything that I hold dear.

That flicker of light in my long lost soul,

Deep inside I do know I am dark and unknown.

I don't know what I want, I don't understand what I deserve,

For things that bother me really stays clinging in here.

Misunderstanding clouds my mind,

Thoughts of you with someone else, before and after

Renders me unkind.

I know it's absurd, but it's my mind,

Complex, fictional and sadly,

never forgets the words you confine.

Little did you say before does stay in mind,

and later attacks at night, connecting dots, Oh my.

It's okay, I shall be fine,

For I wish to live and make you mine.

I lay awake tonight,

Thinking of everything, that's not right.

One night

Loving you was the sweetest part,

Seeing you, made my heart fly.

Your eyes, your smile

One in a million, best in life.

You got bored of me, I didn't.

I just loved you, all day and night.

Reasons made no sense,

Now love seems pointless.

Mine

Through the words,

I lay the deepest of my insights,

my feelings and my fears all combined.

Through my words I convey,

what I can't but what I want to say.

Love the words that don't lie,

those that shine and rise up high.

It's the journey of souls, of two lives,

from unknown to the known, it keeps changing

Yet, stays forever mine.

Day Night

Sometimes in the Night,

I do think of you.

Sometimes in the day,

I still think of you.

And Night and Day, yes I do,

I think of you.

My love for you,

shall stay forever true.

Nothing in the word,

Nothing in my life,

shall pierce the love,

that I have for you.

Despair

It's okay to be sad,
Look back and cry.
Stay blank and be lonely,
do whatever I feel is right.
It's not the regret that I face,
It's the burden, and you won't understand.
For, you are too much of a child and
there's not much to tell.
Ignorant, and buried I keep these,
the reasons and situations.
Sometimes it comes back on,
without any warnings and self treason.
That's when it is necessary
to act, to behave normal.
You won't understand what is inside, and
what is outside, apart from my reasons.
Life's just a play,
for some, it's just a pass, while
for other, it just lasts.
For me, it never seems to end.
Blink that eye, I won't lie and
please cease my existence,
I want to fly high.

Lying the lies

I am feeling nothing,

maybe because I am high

Here I am writing a poem,

Lying all the lie lies.

I have been talking so happy,

with a big smile.

Yes, I am doing great,

that's what I have been saying all night.

Run

When you feel low,

don't you cry.

Stay up high,

'cause it is Do or DIe.

Yes, it is unjust, it's not fair,

but where is the fun,

if you just can't run.

Run from the pain, run from the work.

I am not telling you to escape,

nor to give up.

I mean run,

run them through with a gun.

It's not the result that you must expect,

it's about the fun that you had.

Life is unjust and it's not fair,

but you must face and

Dare to run, without a second guess.

Sometimes

It's unusual, yet so real.

You think you moved on, but

it just comes back on.

Feelings right?

Shut them all off,

tell yourself that you don't care, and

move on from here.

Life was good before,

life can now.

Just get over it, Dream it on,

Please begone.

Don't be sad, don't you cry inside.

It never mattered and it never will.

You simply need to move on.

All is here

It's unusual, yet so real.

You think you moved on, but

it just comes back on.

Feelings right?

Shut them all off,

tell yourself that you don't care, and

move on from here.

Life was good before,   .

life can now.

Just get over it, Dream it on,

Please begone.

Don't be sad, don't you cry inside.

It never mattered and it never will.

You simply need to move on.

Ask me

Ask me a reason,

I will tell you a tale,

A tale about her,

How I met her and

how I lost her.

She might be gone,

But her essence prolongs,

It's the day of nearing,

A moment of forgiving.

A moment of celebration, once this day was.

Now it's a carcass of pretentious joy.

Ignorance

He sat on that bench,

The one where he last met her.

Looking at his right,

He imagined her.

Lost at the beautiful sight of a sunset, she was.

He got closer, remembering the moment

when he first kissed her.

Now, this sunset seems gloomy,

A painful and sad memory.

He got up, wiped his tears,

Walked down the path, still remembering her.

Wrong

"What's wrong?" he asked
for the reasons, he wanted to know.
Ignorance is bliss, that's how it all flows.
Change is what she disliked, yet
She has changed somehow, to someone
he can now never know.

What's wrong, the perfect you.
Influence has changed and he knew.
She out there won't know until
the time is up, and life's not the same anymore.
Somehow he holds, she won't know.
That beautiful smile, those eyes, and playful mind
she forgot, but he won't.
It's not "What's wrong?",
It's "Where's You?"

"Will you find him the same, when
You get back and he has gone too?"

Same Path

He sat on that bench,

The one where he last met her.

Looking at his right,

He imagined her.

Lost at the beautiful sight of sunset, she was.

He got closer, remembering the moment

when he first kissed her.

Now this sunset seems gloomy,

A painful and a sad memory.

He got up, wiped his tears,

Walked down the path, still remembering her.

Canvas

She came into his life with a thousand colors,

For he was a faded canvas.

She painted his life, for once he felt alive.

He loves the art, but forgets to keep it up,

For he is just like an empty canvas,

Waiting to be redrawn.

Thousand colors she left behind,

and no brush in sight.

It's her story not his, it's his daylight.

For he shall now forever stay

An empty canvas till he finds her, the unknown.

No better

When it's this time and I wake up at night,

I imagine you beside me, and I hold you tight.

The feeling of comfort, the sweet beauty of life.

I feel safe, for I promised to keep you safe.

I imagine you just being there,

with hugs and love of yours,

I feel fine, I can rest again now.

For tomorrow's a different day, and

Maybe it's going to be fine.

I hope you to be there,

For you are my sweet love and
I need no better.

Be Mine

She used to love talking to me,

Walk the nights, feel the words.

She used to hold my hand, when

it was dark or she needed a friend by side.

She used to miss me,

The ways I never forgot to miss her,

play games with me that I never heard of,

She used to be always there for me.

She used to make my heart lighter

with her smile, and endless talks, beautiful eyes.

She used to, she used to, be mine.

Long Time

He feels the warmth,

The happiness and the sweetness in his heart.

Thinking about her,

Looking at her pictures,

He imagines his life with her.

He feels the need to kiss her, and

Tell her how beautiful she is.

Tell her how important she is.

That sweet feeling of love,

the stare of her shiny eyes

He loves her the most, and these aren't lies.

For she has his everything, and

She is everything to him.

He would love her forever.

Forever is a long time, but

He wouldn't mind it with her.

A meet in the rain

It was that rain in July,

where she first got to know him.

He was standing in the rain, and

She saw him.

Looking at his happy face,

She saw that child in him.

Closing her umbrella, she joined him.

That moment she fell in love with him,

Playing with him, holding his hand

she started to fill the missing part of him.

That's the day, she found warmth,

she found love, and he became her world.

For him, she was a passing by,

a friend he needed, someone to live by.

He didn't understand much, but

He knew she was all he needed that time.

Fate

Not everything matters, there isn't much to share.

He sat out as the days were approaching and

she was nowhere, o dear.

Dreams are fake, he claimed,

Her voice was his only escape.

His love is fake, she says. O love, why won't you just understand: he isn't a fake.

Depth at which he feels, only two knows of his;

One who is gone, one who failed him.

He just wanted her, not her body but her soul.

Maybe that was too much, and his past haunts,

For it's his cursed fate to find that love no more.

She is there, he loves her but he no longer finds his love that he once had for her.

She is now a stranger to him, his home is lost to him.

O love, what have you done.

He wishes he could find her in Her, again.

Sorry

Everything I have,

I have because of you.

Things that happen,

happens through you.

My life, my wonders are possible

just because of you,

you are my hope

in this dream

that might never be true.

I wish I was there,

to be with you,

when you needed someone to help you.

I was afraid, I am a coward,

and I am sorry for that too.

Wrong journey

Journey to the next day

feels like the continuation of the previous.

Hoping it to be a new day,

I believed I moved past what it was.

Seeing her at times takes me back.

When everything seemed familiar,

and life started to make sense again.

Certain things take time to heal

I made myself believe, but

I wonder how long moving from love needs.

I miss her daily, and I wish things were different,

wish I could say them to her directly.

I loved her wrongly, yet I still did,

perhaps time could have corrected me.

Drowning in work, I try my best but

an unknown pain often haunts me.

sleepness nights, the disturbed mind breaks me.

Not being lesser, nor being higher,

I believed her words, even when I knew

she will certainly get bored of me.

Was it worth to be, when I knew the consequences,

I just believed in being happy, and

for a while, I truly was, selfishly so,
but I loved her wrongly, yet I still did.

Nobody

He was nobody,

With the belief that he could be.

Listened to her reasons,

Loved her the most,

Others aside, he made her his world.

She didn't give it a chance,

Assumed the misunderstanding part,

His love for her in vain,

She wants to go back, and

Left him alone, all again.

Every night

Every day he goes to sleep,

at a time "proper" to him.

Hoping the light of the next day, but

haunted are his dreams,

Reality is much simpler,

sweeter is being awake.

Those dreams as he closes his eyes

enough to make him realize

his worth as a being.

A poor choice for others, a rotten mind,

a seeker, an unlovable being to despise.

Reality is far different, dreams state the truth.

He better gets some sleep,

because it's time again to dream.

Every day

It's odd you know,

When he first saw her, he wasn't attracted.

Yet, he wanted to be with her.

He didn't even know her,

and she was a complete stranger.

Yet, he fell in love with her at first sight,

He didn't understand it, he questioned why.

But later he realized,

For him, it's her every time, every lifetime.

She needs no reason to be loved,

It's just the way she is,

No matter what, he will find her every time.

Every time

It's odd you know ,

When he first saw her, he wasn't attracted.

Yet, he wanted to be with her.

He didn't even know her,

and she was a complete stranger.

Yet, he fell in love with her in the first sight,

He didn't understand it, he questioned why.

But later he realized,

For him it's her everytime, every lifetime.

She needs no reason to be loved,

It's just the way she is,

No matter what, he will find her everytime.

Unhappiness

Sometimes I wish to call you up,

listen to your voice and the sweetness of laughs.

Sometimes I wish to ask you again,

"You still there? let's talk"

Sometimes when I am trying to move,

I see you again and it takes me all back.

Sometimes I wish to tell you,

even though there's nothing called love

I love you for no reason.

Often I want to hold you, and

fall asleep.

Unreasonable thoughts, unreasonable words,

maybe I got it all wrong.

One sentence it all took,

misguides, misleads you overlooked.

Every day I wish,

everything is just a dream, and

may I not wake up in the reality of things.

Sometimes I wish,

promises were true, and

love was real, things were beautiful and

one would not create their own unhappiness.

Close my Eyes

Today I closed my eyes, and

I had a dream that discarded my life.

It all repeated itself and

I was living in an old hell,

it all seemed too real.

It wasn't the first time, but

this time it was all alive.

Aches and reasons,

memories and images combined,

I felt I was ready to die,

today when I closed my eyes."

Thousand words

He had a thousand words to express his feelings,

Emotions that he didn't want to explain.

She made him word them up, but can never understand.

For now, he shall enjoy himself,

selfish and being selfless as someone once said.

Sadness turned into anger, heavy heart got heavier,

Now it's being alone, he shall prefer.

They revolved around themselves,

Negligence to him, but own selves

Setting his heart underneath, for they claimed better.

Understanding their own, considering his later,

For he always put them first, now never.

He shall do the same, unknowingly yet properly.

For he can love himself, he needs none,

Alone is what he preferred, so alone he shall now be on.

Feelings

I have feelings,
Feelings that I want to share,
but the sad truth is that
Nobody would care.

I just want to fly,
fly so high,
With the birds, in the big old sky.
And when it's time,
I want to fall,
Fall so hard, and get deeply hurt.

It's her words that makes me fall,
It's her works that makes me rise,
Is it a crime,
To fall in the first sight?

Alright, I have said enough,
Enough about her,
Enough about the way it feels,
when I am around her.
It feels warm, it feels shy.
This makes me think,
I should just die.

Changes

It now seems like a long time ago,

when things were truly fine.

Non pretentious moments,

love at heart, sweetness in eyes and

that's the place where it all resides.

Wonder what had happened,

words or fictions 'cause before the end

I sensed your reasons.

Irritations you felt when I was near,

the drift of being away,

I wondered if some else planted in your mind that way.

Being not there wasn't a perk,

Never realised what drove us apart.

Did someone reason to you?

or did it all reason to you?

I could never sense it,

Perhaps you could have just bought it to me.

Clearing your mind, have you reasoned a while?

Never asked for you to care,

Perhaps only if you shared.

I act ways to understand what it all means, but

I haven't been bad that way.
You often had wrong versions of me,
when I was harsh I could see.
Calm me down and reason with me,
Never wanted your support,
Just wanted you to be with me.

Unknowing reasons

Why does it hurt so much,
Why do I cry inside?
I have none to lose, yet
I feel so empty inside.

My life ain't sad,
Nor is it empty.
But I feel dead and sad,
Every day and night.

I know I am none,
I know I don't matter,
I just sometimes wish,
Someone would a bit care.

Yes, I got lots, but
None to share,
A lot to say,
But none to care.

I wish I was happy,
Like I think I am.
I wish I could be,
Who I really am.

Empty

This feeling inside me,
Makes me so empty.
I want to feel the reality,
And I do feel guilty.

Tell her that I loved her,
Tell her that I did care,
I wish I was able to
But I need go away far.

Yesterday I decided,
Tomorrow I will tell her,
How I feel and How I want her,
but you see, it's not that simple
When you realise that
There's already another for her.

I am not sad,
I don't want to cry,
I will just suppress this,
And let all my emotions die."

Avoid

I should just avoid her,

'cause I am falling for her.

I know it hurts,

and she won't see me as I see her.

It pains,

It hurts,

My heart bleeds even in the brightest stars,

But I know I will get over this,

'cause I know pain,

I know how to forget just like rain.

But falling for her,

Is the best feeling I ever had,

And this does make me sad

I cry deep inside,

Where none can see,

Sometimes I wish I could just flee.

My mind knows it's true,

But my heart doesn't follow,

I wish I told,

But I know how it would unfold.

So,

I should just avoid her,

'cause I am falling for her.

I know it hurts,

and won't see me as I see her.

Open your eyes

Often, I hold onto words and feelings,

hoping for a new day, I go on listening.

As the days pass by, I realize

things that seem the way should never be,

and sometimes losing hope is a must be.\

Not a day goes quietly,

out of blurry and starry I seem to have found clarity.

No more words to be spared, non to be spoken,

one step closer, now four steps back.

Reasons and thoughts aside,

some made no sense, but something does phase.

Dates get nearer and feelings do reside,

words and all, must be like flies.

It was just a bad dream,

open your eyes.

Long Gone

To the soul long gone,

Thank you.

For all the lessons you taught me,

for all the reasons you gave me,

and for all the letters you wrote me.

To the soul long gone,

Thank you.

For putting up with me,

even when I was scarce.

For holding my hand, and telling

that everything will be alright in the end.

To the soul long gone,

Thank you.

Even when I couldn't be there for you,

You left me with a mind worthy of the world.

Even when things spiralled,

You gave me the strength to hold on.

To the soul long gone,

Thank you, for everything.

Remembrance

Twice a year,

I remember you fondly.

For all the reasons you had, and

for all the things that you did.

Every year when the second arrives,

I tend to miss you deeply,

for it might have been in my power

to help you when you needed me.

Drowning in the thoughts is never the way

you taught me,

out of all the things, I regret some deeply.

I apologize again, till the end of time I shall.

No more twice, no more tears,

I shall remember that you are here,

Still with me.

Meant to be

I often look up to the sky,

and let myself wander.

Sometimes blue, sometimes dark,

but calm and soft,

together with the clouds.

It does make sound sometimes,

but often brings joy.

A place for the birds and

countless lives, seen and unseen there.

Just like the land,

that blue sky loves the world here.

I look at the sky, and

try to understand what it always told me,

to learn the depth in it,

live with the memories but

learn from it.

Be clear as it, be cloudy when meant to be,

love the clouds the way it's supposed to be and

just let things be.

Be free, be boundless,

live the way it's meant to be.

Realization

Some time ago,

I thought being a nobody is sin.

A while ago,

I thought being somebody is a blessing.

Not so long ago,

I realized that unknowingly I am just a toxic person.

Lately,

I understand being nobody has its own value.

Now,

I realize life is much more than what I saw.

Finally,

I decide to be a human with no motives.

Be peaceful and love the world the way it is.

Grudges has no meanings,

Hatred and sadness are just choices of the morally poor.

Happiness is a blessing, compassion is the way and

Blissfulness the motto of life itself and

Time like a stream, keeps on flowing

Unfolding the mysteries of the universe

Forgive

I have always kept notes of my days,

days of overwhelming sadness and

the days of fruitful joy.

Noted them word by word,

unbiased and unheard.

Sometimes I flip those pages, and

a sense of wording strikes,

how something made sense and

now no longer that suffice.

I flip through them and

I realize,

things aren't the way they seem,

people do change and differ.

Humanity lacks forgiveness, and

it's time for me to learn to offer.

There's beauty in the littlest of things,

most of us often never see it.

Sweetness, happiness a part of it, and

appreciation is the greater gift.

For me, it's time to loosen that grip, and

finally, learn to forgive.

Uncertainity

How should it feel

when every time you close your eyes,

and you see her face?

How must it be like,

when dreams are unparalleled,

and sweeter than life?

Do you wait to leave or exit the way out?

the wait can result in a pass out, and

exits are uncertain but you lost somehow.

Passed out dreams without a wish to awake,

should you keep dreaming or smile around?

Tell me, sweet uncertainty,

is it I or unparalleled life is sweeter now, and

closing the eyes feels better, now.

Once a part of life

Lying on my bed,

staring at the ceiling,

noises in my head

directing me out of that feeling.

Awake till I pass out quick,

else the dreams sour and sweet.

Never assume,

without me knowing.

High in the head, sweetness at heart,

unknown truth: is it art?

Unanswered questions,

sweet illusions,

knowing the hidden

does it set me apart?

Rushes of life, reasons unsaid,

one spoken, others stayed hidden.

Uncleared words, unspoken thoughts,

haunted heart with a sweet smile,

unspoken but known

once a beautiful part of life.

Smile

It's a time to smile,

to be happy and to learn.

Life happens, you happened,

I happened, you learn, I learnt.

Thankful for life and thankful for the reasons.

Things go on, life goes on

Sweetness, bitterness, a part of life

Acceptance seems a part of it.

Let it flow and with no grudge,

embrace the beauty of everything,

for it is like a stream,

what's inside shapes the outside,

embrace everything.

Myself

Now I wish lesser,

think less,

do what I want,

and live the best I can.

Weird, even for me to be this,

but I used to be happy

when I wasn't just sad.

Caught up in life,

I forgot the way I was,

past made me anxious and

experiences made me nervous.

I lost myself on the way,

living for someone,

whose life was long over.

I carried a burden, and

lost my life in those thoughts.

Forgetting myself, I frustrated my life,

took one last push, instead of the fall

I pull myself back to life.

I am happy but

the cost was high,

no longer can tell that you are mine.

Now, I wish lesser and with time,

I feel my life.

A Good Day

Not every day is a good day,

Live anyway.

Not all you love will love you back,

still love anyway.

Not everyone will tell you the truth,

Be honest anyway.

Not all deals are fair,

play fair anyway.

Not all beings understand you,

Understand them anyway.

One day you might be lost, but

you shall find yourself again someway.

Not everyone can forgive, so

you must forgive someway.

People shall hide from you,

respect their choices anyway.

Not everyone is good, so

Be good anyway.

Someone might matter to you

more than you do to them,

Just be happy all the way.

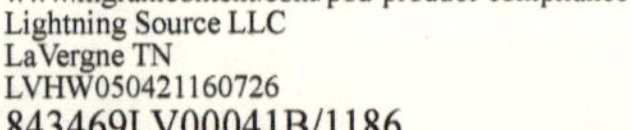